Published by Ad Hoc Fiction.
www.AdHocFiction.com

Purchasing Information:
Paperback available from www.AdHocFiction.com
E-book available from all usual outlets.

Printed in the United Kingdom.
First Printing 2023.

ISBN paperback 978-1-915247-46-9
ISBN e-Book 978-1-915247-47-6

The Top Road

by

Fiona McKay

AdHoc Fiction

To Declan and Jane – you are my people, always.

Contents

Bone

In school, all throughout May and June, the talk is of holidays – Spain, Portugal, Disneyland. Joe keeps quiet. Some of those boasting about where they are going have fathers who are farmers like his da, and Joe knows they must be lying, because you can't leave a farm and go on holiday for two weeks. And there wouldn't be the money for a holiday and to pay someone to see to the cattle. But Pat will look in for the few days they're away, and his da will do the same for Pat later in the summer. That's the plan, anyway.

Kerry is boring. It rains for two of the days, and they are stuck in the car driving all day. They took his mam's car, the one with the two rows of seats in the back, so at least he doesn't have to sit wedged in between his sisters. He had asked his mam for the iPad, to watch something, but she had told him to look out the windows at the beautiful scenery, and he had rolled his eyes so hard they had hurt. The rain blurs everything outside into grey – lashing sea, hard stone, and trees so bent-over they remind him of his granny. Not the one that lives with them, the other one, the one who lives in the nursing home that smells like soup and hospitals.

The day before they are to go home, the sun comes out. His mother says that this would have been the perfect weather for driving The Ring, but he is glad. Long boring drives might as well be on rainy days, and now they can go to the beach. He can't remember the last time he's been to a beach.

It's not like he expected. In his head, it was going to be full of families, lots of other eleven- and twelve-year-old boys, and they'd start playing football together, then something would happen – he hadn't worked out what, but maybe a thief would steal someone's bag – and they would become a gang and hunt down the thief, fight him, get the woman's bag back, and she would be so grateful, she would give them all fivers that they would spend on ice cream and rare Pokémon cards in the shop.

There are no other families on the beach – no other people at all, and certainly no shop – and with that, his excitement disappears, and he feels as flat and stale as the 7Up in the bottle he'd left forgotten in his schoolbag over mid-term break.

After they eat the sandwiches, his mam closes her eyes and tells them they aren't allowed back in the water for at least an hour. Da goes around them all with the bottle of sunscreen, smearing them with the thick white cream, warning them to stop rolling in the sand, it will scratch it right off again and they'll burn. Joe isn't worried. His arms and legs are brown from being outside all summer. And he's not pretending to be a mermaid, like the twins. He calls out that he's going for a walk, and heads down the beach, away from them all.

He climbs some rough rocks, comes to another stretch of beach. From where they had eaten their picnic, they had been able to see the muddy cliffs that break sheer down to the beach. Small clouds drift low over the bright-green grass at the top of the cliffs, blending with the sheep clumped in groups, heads down, chomping away. The girls had asked how come the sheep didn't fall over the edge of the cliff, and his mam had jumped in to say that the sheep were very well behaved and didn't go near the edge, like their mammies warned them, and that's why they didn't fall down. He had laughed, and she had given him a glare, meaning he had to go along with it; meaning it was an important lesson for his sisters. Teacher-voice. Teacher-glare. He prefers her Mam-voice.

It's so quiet. Now and then, he can hear sounds from the top of the cliffs, deep baas from the sheep in their different voices, saying who-knows-what to each other. He walks to the edge of the water, letting it ripple over his feet. Nearby, he sees something gleaming white, splashes his way over to it. In the wet sand is a curly-horned skull, stripped back to the bone, not a shred of flesh left on it. It no longer looks like something that had once been alive, had once eaten bright-green grass, had breathed. He looks up at the cliffs again. And wonders where the rest of its body has gone, what has eaten away all the flesh, and wool, and the bloody insides he knows from the farmyard. One sheep that hadn't listened to its mammy, he thinks, and shivers, a cloud blotting out the sun.

From over the rocks, his da's voice comes, getting louder, looking for him. And his mam too. His insides freeze, knowing he'll be in trouble now, for going too far, being gone too long: all his usual sins. Being a bad example to his sisters. He drops the skull back into the water and runs back as fast as he can, scrambling over the rocks, grazing his hands, ignoring the bright red droplets of his blood. He's too busy trying to reverse time to notice the pain.

Mother-in-Law's Tongue

Eimear feels sweat gather under her arms and behind her knees as she carries the heavy shopping bags in from the boot of the car. The twins run ahead of her into the house, squealing. Joe hangs back, offers to carry a bag for her, but she's used the big, stiff Lidl totes, and they're too heavy for him to carry with grazed palms. She tries not to see his embarrassment, asks him, instead, to go on in and clear the table so she can put the bags down. He gives her a look, and she's careful to keep her face neutral, and anyway, she really does need him to do it. The girls would be willing, but like everything, would make more mess than they'd tidy. She knows she has to let them, has to find the patience for it, but not today, just not today.

When Eimear struggles in, Siobhán is at the table drinking a cup of tea in the rose-patterned china cup and saucer she insists on. Eimear tamps down her impatience, seeing Joe trying to make space around his grandmother, who doesn't move, or help.

'Isn't it great to be on holidays,' Siobhán says, taking another sip. Still annoyed about them going to Kerry without her.

Eimear doesn't reply. It's nice not to have the early starts, getting Ella and Ava into their uniforms, making breakfast for everyone, driving them to school, all the while going over her lesson plan in her head. It's not like she hasn't work to do, though. Joe is fairly self-sufficient, but the girls still need her so much. Tom is still up early and out to the cows. And Siobhán still expects her cup of tea and slice of toast on a tray at eight sharp, or it's death by a thousand sharp remarks all day. I am a smooth grey rock, Eimear thinks, and nothing shall stick to me. She shoos the kids out into the sunshine and puts away the messages without help.

It's petty, Eimear thinks, as she adds chilli and garlic to oil and soy sauce, mixing it into the beef strips to marinate. Her mother-in-law doesn't like spicy food, so Eimear makes it any time she's feeling particularly irritated. The kids love it, and that's her alibi. She smiles to herself, causing Siobhán to ask what's funny.

'Oh, nothing,' Eimear replies. 'Just thinking how nice a day it is – we might have dinner in the garden, the kids love that.' She smiles again at Siobhán's suppressed annoyance, repents by setting out Siobhán's favourite chair in the garden, the lounger that tilts back. She has to drag it out of the back of the shed and wipe down the cobwebs. But it's worth it.

Later, when Eimear's preparing to cook the dinner, Siobhán comes in out of the garden, saying she must give her a hand. It's a hand Eimear doesn't want, because it's never to do something she actually needs. Siobhán parks herself against the kitchen cabinets, between the cooker and the fridge, so Eimear has to keep stepping around her. She knows what will happen if she asks Siobhán to sit down, or just to move out of that spot, and she's not in the mood for dealing with sulks.

She heats the pan as she chops bright-green cabbage, yellow peppers, dark red cherry tomatoes, splashes in sesame oil for its fragrant sizzle. The garlic and fresh ginger are minced into small piles of fire. The dish of marinating beef is glossy with oil. The noodles are ready to slide into the saucepan of boiling water.

'Did you salt the meat,' Siobhán asks. Always asks. Nothing ever has enough salt for her, despite her blood pressure.

'I'll season as I go,' Eimear says. Calmly.

'That's not the way to do it,' Siobhán huffs. 'You salt it at the beginning, rub it in.'

'Not for beef, though,' Eimear says. Calmly. 'If I salt it now, it'll draw the moisture out of the beef. And we want the moisture in the beef. Not in the pan, where it will cool things down and everything will wilt. Which we don't want in a stir-fry.'

Siobhán sniffs loudly and looks away, mouth in a tight line.

Eimear ignores it. 'Dinner soon,' she calls out the back door, and calls again when she sees the twins sitting near the old pump where the ground is always wet. They're 'making dinner' with handfuls of mud, and Eimear roars at them to get in and start scrubbing their hands, now, this instant, no they can't have five more minutes. Tom is coming across the yard, and he steps in to tell them to come with him, and they'll all wash up together.

Eimear ducks back into the kitchen, to see Siobhán scattering salt over the marinating meat, pushing her hands into the oily mass to spread it evenly.

'There,' Siobhán says, and busies herself at the sink, soaping and rinsing her hands. Eimear walks straight back out into the garden, where Joe is nudging a football around, hands in pockets. She does the breathing thing from her app, in for four, hold for four, out for four, hold. After a few goes, she tells Joe dinner in ten minutes and goes back into the kitchen. She slides the meat into the hot oil, pushes it around to cook evenly, drops the noodles into the boiling water. In go the sliced vegetables, the aroma of spices expanding outwards like the universe. She plates the food quickly, then rinses a red chilli from the fridge, holds it in her hand, considering it. Tom steps in, covers her hand with his. 'Not worth it,' he says with a wink. Her heart lifts and her temper cools.

'Dinner,' she calls. Calmly.

A Fox in the Night

Orange, scarlet, red, brown. Fox doesn't know these words, but it knows what it is. A whisk of russet, white-tipped brush, curling around itself like warmth, like companionship, like love.

Humans are something to be afraid of. A universal understanding. Their kits: more complicated. Some would watch, some frisk and play. Some throw stones. No way to know which from which except to fear first, then cautiously learn each kit. Like themselves. Some dangerous, some not.

Night is quiet time. Fewer humans, but not altogether none. Rarely the kits, but sometimes. Fox sniffs the air, taking in the summer-sweet scents of flowering plants, fresh green leaves, dry soil crinkling underneath. There is little of that smell that humans make when they move fast, rolling along: a wrong smell, a not-earth smell. Fox's nose twitches as mice dart through the tall grasses, voles make their way to water. Dinner. Fox stretches out a paw, quivering to run. Something moves in the trees, and Fox's senses say it's human.

Such a very moonlight time for a human to be in the trees. Fox drops the quivering paw, turns tail in a bright flash of colour, and quickly paws away.

Keeping to the hedges and the ditches, Fox lopes silently to the front of the big house, stands, paw raised and ready to run. The night is dark but the moon is so full it's like silver day. Fox watches the house, and a curtain is pulled back. Fox watches the window, and, watching back, is a boy.

Somnambulist

Joe stands by the window. Outside, it is dark and he doesn't know why he's here, and not in his bed. He knows his mam and da will be mad at him if they find him out of bed; knows too that it's the worried kind of mad, not the cross kind. He shouldn't be up, but he can't help it, can't help ending up where he's not meant to be, when he's asleep. When he walks.

He looks down at himself and notices he's wearing his GAA jersey in the county colours, the gold, bright in the moonlight, the blue, slinking back into the shadows. He can't quite understand it – when he went to bed, he was wearing pyjamas, stupid pyjamas his granny had bought for his birthday, like anyone ever wanted pyjamas as a present, and definitely not ones with Spider-Man on them. Maybe he put on the jersey to cover them up, embarrassed even in sleep.

A movement outside the window pulls at the edge of his attention, and he looks out again. The moon is out full now, and it's nearly bright as day out there. The thing that has moved, the thing that has caught his eye, is a fox, standing proud on the tarmac driveway of their house, standing right in the middle, looking straight at him. His dad would say the fox didn't really see him, is just looking at the house, or at the movement of the curtain – he notices he has the raised curtain in his hand – but Joe knows that the fox is looking at him and not the house, not the movement. Their eyes meet, and it is like falling down the last step of the stairs in the dark. The fox is telling him something, but he has no clue what. Maybe he moves, or the curtain moves, or maybe there's a noise, but the fox's ears go up, and it bounds off into the night, stopping once to look back to where Joe stands, still watching.

Choose Your Own Adventure

Joe pushes open his window slowly, so as not to make any noise. It's easier for him than his friend Paudie, who has to sneak down the stairs and open the back door. Joe's house is a bungalow, and his bedroom looks out the front, over the driveway, not out over the yard in the back where Lucky is chained up for the night. Lucky doesn't like to be chained, but he can't be let loose in case he gets out. Some of the farms around here have a few sheep, and Da can't take the chance of having the dog worry them. Worrying them means attacking them, Joe knows. Worrying them sounds so gentle a word for it, like the dog would give them difficult sums to do, not tear their throats open. He heard Da saying that to Paudie's father once, and the picture still comes into his mind sometimes, small, woolly sheep, their white fleeces dirtied from the fields, now drenched in red blood. It's a picture that's hard to get out of his head, once it gets in.

The night is bright with an almost-full moon. It's like a strange kind of daylight, like if the world was in black-and-white like the old movies his granny likes to watch. He makes his way up the driveway and along the road, keeping to the ditch, dry now that it's summer. The dog doesn't stir, doesn't bark. He swings his hurley at the longer weeds and grasses, getting into a rhythm with it. The hurley is to protect himself if anything bad happens. He doesn't imagine what that might be, pushes away the image of the bloodied sheep, keeps walking, keeps swinging.

When he gets near to the place they'd agreed on, there's no sign of Paudie, but he hears a low whistle that makes his heart hurt, beating like the wings of the bird that flew into the kitchen one day, until he realises it's Paudie whistling, and he can breathe again. The pond is like a black disc in the darkness, and Paudie is already set up with the bamboo canes and string they'd scrabbled together from home. He has some bread tied onto the end of it, and dips it into the water while Joe takes out his fishing things from where he'd hidden them in the bushes. It's quiet, but there are small noises all around that terrify and soothe them. They're not alone, and so far, there's nothing really scary, not even a fish.

They muck around for a while, don't catch anything, get their feet wet. Paudie pushes him, pretends he's going to push him in, and Joe whisper-swears at him, loud in the moonlight. No stupid stuff, or he'll tell his da, and then they won't get out again, the grown-ups will put a stop to it. Paudie relents, and they sit on a fallen log, make plans for another night, before making their quiet way back to their homes.

It's going to be the best summer ever.

Fox Hunt

Fox's snout whiffles. The breeze is light, from the south, and on it are tantalising scents: feathers, bone, meat. Fox treads delicately, hind paws stepping neatly into the place the front ones have just vacated. The movement is silent; twigs don't snap, undergrowth doesn't rustle. Fox knows that there are mice and voles to be found nearby, but the finding is work, and fox is tired. Kits take up much energy. The mice can be left for the hissing striped-orange cat that haunts the yard.

Fox noses towards the fence-wire around the small wooden hut. This is not the cat's domain, though this is a time for the cat to be awake. Fox paws the wire, pulling it free of the dry soil, noses under it, coat combed by the metal, small russet strands snagged from Fox's back, hooked on the fence like a calling card; like evidence.

Pacing now, Fox feels the excitement build, ears working to triangulate the snuffling sounds from inside the hut. It is important not to rush this, Fox knows from experience. Any loud squawking from inside the hut will lead to cascades of barks from the black-and-white dog chained up in the yard, lights appearing in the dark house, humans.

Fox pours up the shallow steps like liquid, to where the hut opens, nudges the wooden bar that keeps it closed. Nudges. Listens. Nudges again. The wood makes a low clatter as it pops out of place, and a small wave of sound comes from inside. The door swings open on oiled hinges. The hens inside are sleeping, feathers fluttering as they breathe, move, settle. Fox pauses. Listens. Rises up. Pounces.

Sharp incisors come down on fragile feathered necks. The taste of blood in Fox's mouth is like all the food ever needed, like euphoria. Laser focus in this scrum of screeching feathers. Another neck. And another. A frenzy of teeth and blood and fur and skin. A blood-lust thumping so loud in Fox's ears that the other noises almost go unheard. Almost. Fox pauses, assesses, rushes the door with a hen by the neck, teeth carelessly clamped. Drags the hen under the fence with a wriggle, races to the place he'll bury the hens for later. The dog is howling, flinging itself against the chain. No humans have lit up the house or come out into the yard yet. Fox goes back for another hen. And another. After that, Fox knows there is no point in returning. Lights are on in the house and the yard, and there is movement, and sound, and danger. Fox slides back into the den for family dinner, everyone tucking into warm and bloody flesh.

Anger Management

When they discover the window open, they think it's the sleepwalking, and Joe is so angry with himself he wants to smash something, wants to take his hurley and sweep it across the stupid dresser in the kitchen with all the stupid old delph on it, smash it all to blue and white smithereens. They take him back to the doctor in Cork, and there's a lot of hush-hush talking inside the office while he's left to swing his legs in the waiting room, and when they get home, Da and Mam sit him down for a chat in the kitchen, while the girls watch a stupid Disney movie with Granny and get to eat sweets. For the moment, they tell him, it will be safer if he sleeps on an air mattress in their room, while they see how the new medicine is working.

And so he's stuck. It's only for a few days, they tell him, and shout at the girls not to be so mean when they call Joe a baby, having to sleep in with Mammy and Daddy, and he swears he'll get revenge on them, take their stupid My Little Pony toys and throw them in the slurry tank, cut their dolls' hair when they're asleep, and then he remembers he won't be able to wander around the silent house at night any more, and he shouts, 'fuck' as loud as he can, and Granny puts her hand to her chest like she's having a heart attack, and Mam says, 'Joe!' very loud, and Da says, 'Come on Joe and help me in the yard,' and they go and hose it down, use the big yard brushes to scoot the water so it doesn't pool on the concrete and when that's done, Joe doesn't feel as though his face is burning any more, or that he wants to shout, but Da starts talking while they're putting away the hose, saying that it's nothing like Joe being a baby, just they want to mind him, can't have him opening the windows in his sleep, or who knows what might happen, it wouldn't be safe. And Joe can't tell him that his summer is ruined now, and all the plans he and Paudie had for exploring, though not fishing again because it was boring and they didn't catch anything, but all the places they wanted to go when there was no one nagging at them to do chores, or play with sisters, no time now when they could just be themselves. He can't tell his da all that.

And later in the summer, after everything, he burns with guilt that if he hadn't forgotten to close his window that night they'd been fishing, if he hadn't been distracted by hearing his granny flush the toilet, hadn't dived back into his bed and pretended sleep until he was asleep, if he hadn't been starving the next morning and in a hurry to get to the kitchen when he smelled rashers frying, if he'd thought up a better reason for the window being open a crack – like, it was too hot, like, 'I opened it in the morning to let out a fart' – anything other than a lame 'I don't know' then maybe he would have been able to get out other nights, and meet Paudie, and bring his hurley, and go on adventures, and everything would have turned out alright.

Fox Listens

To human ears, the cry sounds like a cat. Hot summer night mating cries. Not the smallest of human kits, unable to walk by themselves, unable to communicate except through cries of varying intensity. Tiny. Defenceless. Humans are sometimes confused, but Fox is not confused. Fox's ears are more alive to the tiniest of sounds, to the meanings of sounds. This was not a cat. This was not a tiny human kit either. But the sound was more human than other, and the russet fur on Fox's neck prickles upright at the sound. This is the sound of fear.

Fox Eternal

Fox noses out of the burrow, circles the water, sniffs the air. Fox smells many things on the warm night air: a dog – the black-and-white one that lives leashed outside the house; field mice – so small and tasty, but fast; fish – in that circle of water, hard to paw out; people – familiar and unfamiliar. Fox's nose twitches, a delicate shudder of whiskers, assessing. Then darts, a quick, bright flash of brush in moonlight.

Nearby, fox passes the slate-roofed white house. Tonight, there is no boy at the window. Tonight, no light calls attention to a window square. All is quiet, but trees moves their limbs in the breeze, grasses and stemmed summer flowers sway, and somewhere, not far, a human is moving outside. Fox ducks out of the moonlight, follows the dry ditch, follows unseen fox-paths to a place of disturbed earth. To a place where the carcass of a chicken rots slowly, awaiting Fox's return. This scent is a delight to Fox. This scent says, kits will be fed. This scent says, tonight is not a night to hunt.

Fox roots in the soil, catches a bone in sharp teeth and pulls, pulls, pulls, until the mess of feathers and meat is free, shakes the dirt off, skitters away home. Meat in mouth, feathers jouncing as Fox lopes along. The scent of old blood and shrinking sinews, of maggots juicy-feasting and alive, of decaying muscle and old entrails. Saliva oozes from Fox's mouth, wets the feathers nearest, dulls the brain and turns up the volume of Fox's hunger, the ravening that will tear this plump hen to bloody shreds. Turns down the other senses, dulls the ears, makes the whiskers forget, as Fox darts and dashes home. The lip of the den is in sight when Fox's bright eye sees something, the dark shine of metal in the air, a tall figure stepping out from the trees, an instrument of metal and wood smashing, smashing, smashing down on Fox's fragile skull. Again and again, splintering bone, spilling blood. Fox's thoughts dance from meat to kits, from the warm and softly scented air to all the pathways of his world, taking him back, back, back, to when he was a small kit in a different den with his own mother, her tail curled around him for warmth and protection, and in his throat there is a sound, as everything becomes blacker than the night, a sound that humans might recognise, as one of their own, crying for home.

Man's Best Friend

Tom takes the call in the yard, drinking a cup of tea he's brought out with him, talking nonsense to the dog. Lucky lets out a small bark, his black-and-white ears twitching upwards.

'Pat,' he says. 'What can I do for you?'

'Any sight of Paudie around your place, Tom? No sign of him here, thought I'd check before I start worrying. Maedhbh is panicking a bit, looked in on him when she came in – she's on nights this week – and he wasn't there. Probably gone out on his bike or something, but you know how the women are...'

'I'll check in with Joe, ring you back,' Tom replies and ends the call. He texts Eimear rather than track dirt into the kitchen. Her reply is quick and he then heads out, out, out, phone to his ear, striding with Lucky running ahead and turning back, his pointed face quizzical in the air.

It would be five minutes in the car to go round the road, but walking is better. He can see more that way. Lucky is supposed to be a sheepdog, maybe he can round Paudie up too? Tom urges him forward, but Lucky's brown eyes keep firmly on him. He's glad of the company.

The going is easy enough. The weather has been mostly dry recently and the muck has dried out here. Nothing to slow him down, suck at his boots. Hard to tell if anyone has been through here. No footprints. He detours past the silage tanks, always a nagging thought, but there's nothing there. He thinks about the pond, and turns his feet, Lucky wheeling around him, sensing where they are going, flying forward, a long streak of black-and-white fur in the sunshine. The innocence of dogs, Tom thinks, striding steadily after.

The pond is cool, not too deep, fed by a trickle of a stream. He'd shown it to Joe only months before, judging him sensible enough to be trusted around water. Sworn him not to tell the girls, and Joe had been only too happy to have this secret place, tucked away behind trees. Hadn't been sworn against telling Paudie though, and Tom wonders. There is always some danger, something to worry about. The pond on his land. The abandoned tunnels on Pat O'Meara's. Always something to keep the kids away from. But this is the childhood Tom had wanted for his children: the freedom he had as a boy, an alternative to videogames and violence.

Eimear had wanted to live in town, when they got married. Closer to the school where she worked. He couldn't just walk away from the land, though. And his mother. Couldn't leave her alone in the house. Farmers don't commute, he had told Eimear.

The pond water is still in the mid-morning heat, and he stops for a minute at an old stump in the cool of the trees. There is mud here, and prints, but to him they don't look new. He has an idea the boys might have come here to fish, though when, he can't say. There had been wet socks, one morning, Eimear giving out yards, and he had said nothing. Lucky runs on ahead of him towards O'Meara's place. Tom follows more slowly, sweeping his gaze over and back, over and back, not knowing what he's looking for, but looking. Lucky pauses to investigate something in the bushes, and Tom goes over, just in case. He thinks he hears rustling but there's nothing there, just some stink, like maybe a fox, and he makes a mental note to fix the latch on the henhouse door – he'd promised Eimear after the fox took her chickens the other night – continues on, looking, looking, looking.

Once O'Meara's yard is in sight, Lucky takes off like a greyhound, hindquarters flashing in the sun, the smooth, natural grace of an animal running. Pat's dog, older, is dignified in his return of Lucky's enthusiastic greeting; still, they both yip a little and move off around the yard to examine the day's smells.

'Any news?' Tom asks.

'Not a thing. He's probably off gallivanting around somewhere, but no sign of him. I'll give him a right sceilp when I find him, giving his mother a fright like this.'

They stand apart, while the dogs move around them, between them. This won't be a time for a cup of tea, a few Kimberley biscuits, their gingery and mallow softness reminding him of childhood. They talk about the land, make a plan to search from there to the top road, from there to the stream, parcelling it out. Tom thinks about the pond. Thinks to ask if Paudie is ever interested in fishing, but the pond is on his land, and he doesn't know how to put it. Maedhbh comes out, shivering in the sun, white and hollow after night duty over at the hospital, and he feels sick to his stomach, thinking how Eimear would be in the same circumstance. Will he mention the pond, ask about wet socks? He opens his mouth, but nothing comes out.

The moment passes and they head off in their separate directions, the dogs running to heel after swift whistles, and Tom heads east, to the stream, covering the ground Pat has already been over, fresh eyes, and all that. And a stone in his chest.

Someone, in the Shadows

The stuff is wearing off now, every part of him screaming for more, but he has nothing. All the stuff he came out here to get, gone. Had he shared it with the fellow selling it? He can't remember. Can't remember anything other than the feeling when the stuff coursed through him. Was it yesterday? The day before? Looks at his wrist but there's no watch there.

Panic crashes through his jumbled thoughts. Something bad, something bad. Has happened. Will happen. Or both. The thought throbs in time with the pain in his head. He hears a voice, a dog barking some way off, eases himself through the bushes, cuts back along the ditch and steps out onto the road. Puts one foot in front of the other. Feet snapping down onto the tarmac like they've nothing to do with him, like he's not controlling them at all. Maybe he's not there, on the road, maybe it's all still a nightmare, maybe those bad things didn't happen the way he thinks.

But every time he closes his eyes, he sees blood. He wishes he had some stuff to take away this pain.

Doubt

Father Murphy sits in the confessional with his knees pressed against the wood of the dividing panel. Built in a time when people were smaller, he thinks. Built in a time when the demand was higher, when the priest sat in the centre, sliding open and closed the grille that let through the words of sin and absolution, a stream of penitents opening and closing the doors on either side. It was busy earlier, after ten o'clock Mass finished. Always a few of the older people queuing up to whisper their petty jealousies in his ear, receive their few Hail Marys. On a visit to Rome in his seminary days, he had seen a confessional where the priest entered through a concealed back door. He wishes that was a possibility now, and that he could slip out to the vestry, put on the kettle for a cup of tea, sit down with a book instead of this waiting.

It's stuffy, though the air in the church is cooler than outside. There are scents of dust and wood, hits of incense-spice and the wood polish the cleaner uses. The breviary is unopened beside him. I could be praying, he thinks, but his mind is unfocused. His thoughts wander, taking the path back down the hill to his younger days, when his knees didn't hurt getting up from the kneeler, when he didn't hear them crunching as he genuflected to the tabernacle. He thinks of the first parochial house he lived in, young priests a rarity even then. He thinks of the parish priest, long dead now. Thinks too of the housekeeper, a woman his own age, married young and husband who knew where, the light summery scent of her perfume, the way her hair curled in towards her neck.

Footsteps, the slam of the door to his left, his least favourite side. He slides open the grille, wondering if he has it in him to listen to any more petty sins. If he were God, there's so much he wouldn't give a damn about. An earthy, dirty smell creeps through the grille, filling the space, filling his mouth. He pulls his stole across his nose, says, 'What is it, my child?' There is silence. Is there a person there, or did someone throw a bag of excrement in and run off? He would have heard the footsteps, wouldn't he?

'Bless me, father, for I have sinned,' a man's voice says, low and hoarse.

Afterwards, he can't say if it was a young voice or older.

Afterwards, he thinks about the seal of the confessional. Thinks about the fact that he can't identify the man, so there's no seal to be broken. He thinks for precisely the length of time it takes him to remove his mobile phone from an inner jacket pocket, and, with fingers that find the job tricky, dials the number for the Garda station. While he waits, he checks over the church. Opens all the confessionals, huffs up the stairs to the choir balcony, looks in the toilets. Then locks the front and back doors. When the Gardaí arrive, he brings them into the vestry and makes tea, holding the mug in his freezing fingers as he recounts, carefully. He tries to remember the exact words, panics when they slide out of his mind. He knows what the man said though, that he had hurt a child. That it might be bad.

The tea is cold in the mug when the Gardaí leave. They're taking it seriously, they say. The lack of detail is a problem, they say, because where are they to start. And it could all be a hoax, of course, they tell him. The smell, the hoarse voice, maybe it's someone suffering a delusion, off their meds. Maybe, Father Murphy agrees, and wishes he could believe it.

It is later in the day when news emerges that young Paudie O'Meara can't be found. The Gardaí have been called in, and neighbours are helping search the farm. The boy hasn't been seen since bedtime the previous evening, so no one knows how long he's been missing. If he is missing, and not just gone off with some friend. But Father Murphy has a bad feeling about it. Gets on his knees at the front of the church, and prays.

In the Shadows by the Road

Walking in the shadows, skirting the town, he comes to the church. He pauses, some memory of childhood pushing through the haze, the pain, sending him through the heavy doors into the soothing dark inside. The need for the stuff isn't as strong in here, in the cool, in the dark. It's like being asleep, only better.

Out of instinct, he slips into the wooden booth. If he is truly sorry, he will be forgiven. He remembers these words. *Bless me, father. For I have sinned.* He has, hasn't he? Something bad. Something to do with a child, but why would there have been a boy out in the middle of the night, in the deep dark? Maybe there was no boy. The wooden board over the fretted grille slides back; there's a sound, like breath being sucked in. He breathes in and catches his own smell. There's fox on him. Maybe it was just the fox? But he thinks about the boy.

'Bless me father, for I have sinned.'

A Bad Night

In the morning, Joe's mam says he looks tired, and asks did he have a good sleep. It's not the usual way she asks, when he looks tired, to find out if he'd walked in his sleep, without actually asking. He'd been stuck sleeping on the stupid air mattress in her room, with her and Da creeping in after watching their television programmes, careful not to wake him. But he had been awake. The stupid medicine the doctor gave him makes him feel awake at night, tired and sleepy during the day. He'd been awake, and trapped. And Paudie will be furious with him.

Anyway, she's all distracted by something on her phone, and only gives him a quick glance.

'Joe,' she says, 'Dad wants to know have you seen Paudie since yesterday? I guess not, you're only just up.'

Then goes back to her phone without waiting for an answer, fingers quickly texting, telling him to keep close to the house, not to talk to strangers. As if.

All day, he keeps thinking about the fox. Probably after the few hens left, but Da said he'd fix the latch after the last time. He keeps looking for a glimpse of rusty orange fur while he's doing his morning chores. He's mainly pushing a brush around, but his da gives him a bit of extra pocket money, so he doesn't mind. He doesn't mind the grassy smell of cow dung. Just as well. With Da not there, he could slack off. The part of summer he loves the most is getting to mooch off by himself, walk through the fields, investigate ditches and hedgerows, and be back in time for dinner. He sighs when he remembers that there won't be any of that at the moment. He has to stay nearby, stay safe for some reason. Maybe they know about him and Paudie going to the pond, about the plans they had for last night.

Protocol on the Recording, Investigation, and Management of Missing Persons – An Garda Síochána Mission Statement

The name, address, telephone number of the person reporting and their relationship to the missing person are given, haltingly, in a voice slurred with fear, with tears held back for later.

A parent, having to make this call, a young Garda, still wet behind the ears, just down from Templemore, answering the phone, his brain automatically pulling up the protocol for the report of missing persons, fingers fumbling the keyboard as he flicks open the document, sends a message to his sergeant sipping morning tea in the next room and pulled, unwillingly, away.

Keeping his voice calm as he asks name and age – eleven, his heart pulls at eleven, it seems so far away, too close – description of all clothing including underwear and footwear.

His sergeant, looming over the desk, putting the call on speaker, announcing himself, shortcircuiting the conversation, back it goes to the beginning: basic details, Paudie, not seen since bedtime, no sign of him on the farm, been over it with a neighbour, with the dogs, sniffing him out, but no luck.

Parents worried. So worried. So completely out of character, and no, he doesn't have a phone, wanted to keep him away from all that online stuff as long as possible, all the things you hear

(crying, in the background, a woman's voice, why hadn't they got him the bloody phone he wanted for his birthday, turning twelve soon, going into sixth class, most of his friends have phones)

'Pat, Maedhbh – John Maher here, we have you on speaker so young Hennessey here can take down the details. Look, don't be worrying, I'm sure he'll turn up safe and sound, you know how young lads are, probably woke up early and went off for a ramble, plenty of space for it.'

A pause, a clearing of the throat for attention – more details to be taken says Hennessey, pointing at his screen.

Maher waving him off, not flippant but dismissive, ignoring the words being mouthed silently at him, written on a scrap of paper – PROTOCOL – middle-aged eyes rolling at the naiveté of youth, of inexperience.

Interruption – 'I'msosorrytherearequestionsweneed-toask' – pulls out the handbook

Maher handflaps at Hennessey and his damn questions. 'Who went over the farm – yourself Pat? And Tom Hogan? You'll need a bit more than the two of you to cover those acres though, so we'll have a little think about that.'

Garda Hennessey puts the call on mute, insists: 'Sir, we have to ask these questions, we have to find out if the boy has run away, is there any reason, any problem at home, we need to be very careful in case there's any abuse or anything going on, need to take all the details now, sir, the protocol is to scale up now and scale down if necessary, all clearly laid out in the mission statement. Sir.'

How to say – I know you know these people, Sir, but you have to proceed as if you don't – and not get transferred out of his first posting?

What if he's wrong though, what if his lack of local knowledge means that this boy regularly rambles off?

What if he's making a fool of himself?

What if he isn't?

What if he fucks this up – pictures himself in front of a disciplinary committee, explaining why he has only sketchy notes of the first interview?

His sweat glands prickle – armpits, groin, the crease behind his knees, hairline – and blood capillaries in his neck flood as the flush spreads up his face.

Sergeant Maher, swells to full height, width – 'Known these people all my life. What the hell are you talking about, ye spailpín, here a wet week.'

'Protocol, sir, sorry sir.'

Maher unmutes the call – 'Listen, Pat, Maedhbh, I'm going to have young Hennessey here take all the details while I head over to you. Don't mind if he asks all sorts, we have to follow the protocols, you know, it's important to get this right from the start, and sure look, if the lad turns up, then all to the good.' Listens, continues – 'No, everyone thinks that, but you don't have to wait twenty-four hours to report a missing person. Sooner the better, really. You did the right thing, absolutely the right thing. I'm heading straight over to you now. I'm putting you back on to Hennessey now, and he'll take all the details.'

Sweat cooling – in his armpits, in his groin – as the sergeant swings on his jacket and makes for the door. 'Mr O'Meara, I'm sorry to have to ask you all these questions. What time last night did you last see your son, Paudie?'
And on down his list, tick box, insert information – shimmering from his screen, the portrait of a young boy appearing, word by word by word. The thrall of fear running through him: how big a child is in the life of a family, how small out in the world.

Lost.

Or taken?

Garda John Hennessey – Notes of Telephone Interview with Pat and Maedhbh O'Meara

File: Patrick (Paudie) O'Meara, Missing

1. Pat O'Meara here, out at Ballygar. I don't know if I need to be contacting you at all, but it's my son, we haven't seen him since he went to bed last night, and we're getting worried.

2. My son, Paudie. Patrick, really, but I'm Patrick, and my father before me was Patrick, so I became Pat, and my fella, he's Paudie, you know, for Padraig, the Irish.

3. Maedhbh, have you any idea what Paudie was wearing? Are his pyjamas in the bed? We didn't see him, so how do we figure this out? What if we're wrong, what if you send out a search party with the wrong information?

4. Ballygar, Co. Tipperary.

5. His bike is still in the yard, so he's not on that. So, no other vehicle. No, I didn't hear any vehicle here last night. You don't think, you don't think someone took him, do you? Like in a van or something?

6. Average height for his age, maybe a bit taller. He's eleven, twelve soon, early next month. Light brown hair, short, but growing out a bit. Blue eyes. A bit of a tan from being around the farm with me since school finished. Build? Ah, ye know, a skinny lad, had a growth spurt there recently, and he's all arms and legs.

7. Maedhbh will have a photo. You can have your pick of the thousands on her phone. Where do we send it?

8. He went off to bed around ten-thirty. Gets to stay up a bit later over the holidays. Wasn't that much later when I went myself – Maedhbh was at work. She's a nurse. Ah no, we wouldn't be looking in on him any more. Lads that age want a bit of privacy from their parents.

9. Usually, Maedhbh would be the one getting him up. For school, like. When she'd be on days more. No, she doesn't bring him to school. Eimear Hogan comes round the road to collect him with her crew. She's a teacher in the school and her lad, Joe, is in the same class. Anyway, now it's the school holidays, Paudie can sleep in. Maedhbh is on nights – she gets more days off that way. I'd be at the milking early, and then I'd have something to eat around ten, and he'd usually be up by then. Wasn't around this morning, but it wasn't until later that I got worried.

10. I know you have to ask all the questions on your list, but what does that even mean? No, he doesn't pose a threat to others.

11. Jesus, no, I hope not. Who would want to harm him? Why would he be with someone who would want to do that?

12. I mean, he's a kid, and kids do wander off, don't they? Lose track of time. But not like this. Jesus, not like this.

13. What I'm hoping is that he woke up when I was out at milking, grabbed himself a bite of food, or something to bring with him, and headed out on an adventure. He's not meant to wander the farm, and he's not meant to go over as far as Hogan's but boys will be boys, won't they? I know he's not with Joe, but maybe he's somewhere on their land, or ours. We've never had a hard border between us. Maybe he'll stroll in totally unconcerned and asking what's for dinner. So that's what I'm hoping. He'll walk back in here and wonder what all the fuss is about. That's what I'm focusing on.

14. We were thinking of a phone for his birthday, what with him going into sixth class and all that. But young Joe Hogan doesn't have one either, so we thought we could hold out for the summer, let him have one last summer as a child, you know, before the whole teenage thing starts up. Wish we'd bought him the damn thing now. Wish we had him microchipped like the bloody cattle, then we could find him easy enough. Jesus. Sorry. It's just, where is he? The world just feels too big. Sorry, just give me a minute there.

15. Yea, no, I'm fine, I'm fine. No, we don't let him use social media. I mean, he's mad into Fortnite and Minecraft and all that. He can message his friends when he's playing a game, but that's it.

No, I can't think of any reason why he would run away. He's a good lad, and there's never any trouble. I mean, there's the usual stuff – we get after him to tidy his room, help more around the house. But he does well in school. He's on the football team, and the hurling. Maedhbh probably talks to him more about feelings, rows with friends, that kind of thing. But he comes to us if there's something bothering him. And I know, at that age, the small stuff feels like big stuff, but it's all small stuff.

Every minute, I'm just hoping I'll put down the phone, and he'll be outside, kicking a ball against the end wall, and mortified that we called the Guards. That's what I'm hoping.

Amber Alert

By lunch time, Joe is bored. He can't say it though. He'll be made to play with his little sisters, or do something helpful for his mother, or worse, his grandmother. Joe hates having to go into her room. It makes him feel like that huge fly he saw all tied up in a spider's web, unable to move. Her room is dusty, and smells of powdery perfume, and wee. There's no way he's telling anyone he is bored. Not that anyone is asking. His da has been over at O'Meara's for hours, looking for something. He's not back yet, and Mam has the lunch waiting on him. Joe can smell it, and he's starving, but he doesn't want to say anything. It feels like the bad part of Christmas in the kitchen, the part where things are being organised and no one has any time, and it feels like the magic is slipping, like there's no magic at all, just Mam up early and cranky as hell.

He slides into the kitchen to see if there's anything he can eat and stands just inside the door. There's a spot where the shadow from the fridge-freezer falls, and he's almost invisible there. It's a good spot for hearing things. After a few minutes, he wishes he weren't there, but doesn't want to draw attention to his presence by moving. The kitchen should be empty, but isn't. Granny and Mam are there, the radio on loud, Granny shushing in that way she does because she can't hear well but his da says she won't admit it. He isn't even making any noise and still she's shushing, sounding really cross, so he stops where he is and waits for whatever's on the radio to finish.

It's the news, and he hates the news, the news is boring, and an amber alert sounds like something to do with the weather, which is even more boring than the news, and it's only when he hears their townland mentioned that he starts to focus and he's going to ask but Granny has a hand in the air like that would stop words in their tracks, and then Mam turns with her phone up to her ear and her face is very, very white, with two bright spots of colour on her cheeks, like a clown, and he knows not to say this out loud because he's learnt that nobody wants to look like a clown, but also because his mother looks upset, there's something wild and loose about her face and he feels cold, cold, cold, like his middle is dropping away, because he's never seen her look like this, never, and he's frozen there, shut out, with Granny still shushing, though he's not the one making noise, and then Mam turns off the radio and says to Granny,

'Oh my God, Siobhán, that's about Paudie, it's Paudie who's missing,' and only then does she notice Joe in the room, and only then does he realise someone's screaming, and that it's him.

Paudie is the missing child and now everything in Joe's stomach – his breakfast toast, the bowl of cereal, a banana, two chocolate biscuits from the tin – wants to come hurling out of his mouth to cover everything his mam is saying in a tidal wave, to stop the words he doesn't want to hear. When Joe sees that she's been crying, it's too much, and he starts crying too, great gouts of tears. He flings off anyone who comes near him. That's when his father arrives in the back door, kicking off his boots, walking across the tiles in his grey socks and catching Joe by the shoulders, saying. 'Enough now, enough now.' Settling him.

Lunch is quiet. He tells his mother he can't eat, but his stomach betrays him, calling for more. Nobody mentions Paudie. His mam and his da both warn him to say nothing in front of the girls, like he needs to be told that. They're still babies, dressing up in princess dresses, believing in stuff like the tooth fairy, fairies in general, and Santa. Leaving fucking glitter everywhere after them, he thinks. He has heard his da saying that, though not in front of Granny. He wouldn't repeat it, but he likes the feel of thinking it. The violence of the words soothes him.

After lunch, with the girls distracted, his parents sit him down to talk, ask questions, before his da heads back out to help with a search party. He ends up running for the bathroom and throwing up what feels like everything he's ever eaten, and still it's not enough. He wants to throw himself up, flush himself away, be gone. Be wherever Paudie is. And bring him back safe.

Darkness Before Dawn

It's too early to be awake, the sky still a dark dusky night blue, but Eimear can't sleep. No one should be able to sleep, she thinks; we should all be out combing the woods, the fields. There's nothing to be done in the dark. Tom is asleep. She grudges it to him, reminds herself he was out on the search all day, that he's exhausted.

She hears something, some movement in the house, and immediately she's alert in a way she can never remember being before the kids. One ear always open. She gets out of bed carefully, so as not to wake Tom, but quickly, because that's what you do when there are kids. And she can smell something that's making her brain think no, no, no, without telling her conscious mind what it is. Hoodie, slippers, and she's making her way down the corridor, sniffing, sniffing, running towards the kitchen. Something sweet – vanilla, maybe? It had better not be the twins, she thinks, wrenching open the door.

It's not the girls. Siobhán has the oven door open, Eimear's big bright oven gloves on, lifting out a tray of something. The kitchen is warm, smells of baking –

a jammy, buttery scent that curdles in Eimear's throat. 'What are you doing up?' she asks.

'Couldn't sleep,' Siobhán says. 'Much like yourself.' She puts down the tray. Jam popovers, a thing she hasn't made in years, her own recipe that's something between pastry and shortbread, jam-filled. She puts two more trays into the oven, sits down at the table when she's done.

Eimear puts on the kettle, makes a pot of tea the way her mother-in-law likes it, joins her at the table.

'I thought I'd make something for the searchers,' Siobhán says. 'You were killt all day making tea yesterday, thought they might need something to go with it. And I couldn't sleep a wink. Better up than tossing and turning.'

'It's a terrible thing,' Eimear says. Tears pull at her throat, the way they have since the news came about Paudie. Siobhán pats her hand, lifts the teapot and refills their cups. All the crying has left Eimear thirsty all the time. All the crying she's had to sneak time for, keeping a bright face on for the kids, for Joe, pale and haunted and unable to sit still, too young to go out with the search parties. Old enough to feel the fear.

'Did I ever tell you,' Siobhán starts, 'about the time Tom went missing? He can't have been more than two or three. Adored his dad, followed him everywhere, when he had the chance. It was some job to keep him inside if he had a mind to go out.'

She pauses, opens the oven door, the fan roaring like a jet engine in the quiet hour.

'Anyway,' she continues, 'he was supposed to be having a nap. He was a busy child and I used to relish it when he'd sleep for a while. I could have a few minutes where I wasn't so totally taken up with what he was doing. There was no noise, so I went in to check on him, and the cot was empty. I screamed, and Tom Senior came running in. I searched the house, and he went running to the silage pit, then the stream, came back empty-handed.' She stops speaking, stares out at the lightening sky.

'Where did you find him?' Eimear prompts.

It takes Siobhán a minute to focus in on her. 'Oh,' she says, with a small laugh. 'The henhouse. He loved collecting the eggs with me, and he'd gone to "help Mammy", he said. He was sitting among the hens, them clucking like mad things, him covered in hen dirt and egg yolk. It felt like the longest hour of my life.'

Eimear puts her hand on Siobhán's. 'I can just imagine, it must have put the heart across you.'

'You can't imagine,' Siobhán snaps, pulls her hand away. 'No one can imagine, unless they've been through it. And no one should go through it. No one.' She takes her cup and bangs it into the sink, goes back to the oven.

Eimear gets up. The light is changing outside, thinning to a pale blue. In the east, the sun is rising, and soon, the search will start again. She doesn't want to wake Tom, but he said he'd be up at five-thirty, to be ready at daybreak. Another day, she thinks, another day of this horror, this not-knowing. No one should have to go through this, she thinks, as she heads back down to the bedroom, the shower already running in the ensuite, the bed empty.

Sunday Mass

'This is the word of the Lord. You may be seated.' Father Murphy waits while those that can, take their seats on the hard, mahogany pews. Many more are standing at the back. There are more outside, gathered in a ring around the entrance of the church. Occasionally through the Mass, the great entrance doors had opened with a clatter, a head poking in to see if there was space inside. There wasn't. He might hope that the church was always this full, but couldn't, not for this reason.

'Our scripture today, from the gospel of Luke, talks of loss. Of a lost sheep. Which of us, the Bible says, with a hundred sheep, upon losing one, would not leave the ninety-nine, and seek out the missing one. And when he finds that one lost sheep, he rejoices, carries it home on his shoulders, calls out to his family and neighbours to rejoice, for that which was lost, has been found.' He pauses in the silence. There isn't a rustle or a cough anywhere.

'Here I will diverge from the parable, which goes on to talk about sinners and righteous people. This is not what I am here to talk about today. Today, the lost sheep in our parish is an innocent lamb. Our lamb has wandered from the fold, and we are all the shepherd. We must all go into the wilderness, into the desert, and search for our lost lamb. Search, and keep searching until we bring our lamb back, and Pat and Maedhbh O'Meara can rejoice with family and neighbours, when that which is lost, is found.'

The O'Mearas are there, sitting at the front, with Tom and Eimear Hogan flanking them. Tom's mother, Siobhán, is in the row behind with the Hogan children, the twin girls who made their First Communion here in the church a few months ago, and Joe, Paudie's friend, the two due to make their Confirmation the following year when they go into sixth class. Joe looks pale and wretched, and no wonder. A terrible business, a child going missing.

There is a great view, from the pulpit, of his community, the ones lined around the walls, the ones he knows are outside. He rests his hands on either side of the lectern, leans forward: one with them.

'I know you all want to help. I know you are all doing your best for Pat and Maedhbh in their time of need. And now I am going to ask you to do more. I'm going to ask you to pray, certainly, but Our Lord was a practical man, a man of action as well as of words. I'm going to ask those of you who are able, to volunteer for the search parties that will be led by the Gardaí.

And I'm going to ask you all to turn your minds to the last forty-eight hours, and anything out of the ordinary that you might have noticed. You may think that you have nothing to contribute, but you might have that one tiny piece of information that is of use. And if there is anything you do know, and you are afraid of speaking out, feel free to come and tell me in confidence. Someone here might know something that could end this hell that Pat and Maedhbh are living through.'

He gets down from the pulpit, busies himself with the rituals for the consecration, the words automatic to his tongue, while his brain flicks through all the faces in the congregation. He matches known voices to faces, wondering, wondering, but can't link anyone to that confession the day before. Maybe one of the men at the back, maybe one of those standing outside in the July heat. Maybe nowhere near the church at all. He raises the host high, recites the prayers, this is his body, this is his blood. And shivers.

The Searchers

They look like convicts, sweeping across the land with their clear plastic sacks and litter-pickers. The blue shoe covers, the plastic gloves – they're different though. Tom moves forward, eyes flicking left and right, every tiny thing that isn't an item in nature, picked up with the picker and deposited in the evidence bag. A line of men and women, grim-faced in the sunshine, an inappropriately beautiful summer day.

So many small pieces of rubbish on the farms. Scraps of paper, frayed to lace by wind, by brambles, by fences. Plastic bags that zoom around like kites in winter, coming to rest in hollows, weighted down by a year of leaves and grass and soil. It's backbreaking work, worse than picking spuds, but he keeps his focus to his own few yards, sweeping his eyes across and back, across and back, while his mind jangles.

The worst of it, Pat and Maedhbh kept to the house by the Gardaí. The shock on their faces when it dawned on them, they weren't being kept there for solace, Pat insisting he'd be fine to help with the search. Kept in the house where the Gardaí could keep an eye on them, just in case.

Ridiculous. They had nothing to do with their son's disappearance. They were broken with grief this morning. Yesterday, when he and Pat had taken a look, it was still in the realm of something that could be explained away, something that could resolve itself into a situation that turned out well, Paudie arriving in the kitchen, starving, showing his father the note he's left, unseen, on the fridge, the table, beside the house phone. There had been no note.

Tom kept thinking, as his feet picked their way across land he was born to, of Pat and Maedhbh, drinking tea in their kitchen with a young Garda. He could feel the pull Pat must be feeling, to be out here, doing something: looking, finding. The years stripped back to when he and Pat were growing up, passing back and forth between the two farmhouses, learning to drive tractors in their early teens, off road, no need for licences. It was the life they wanted for their own sons, and Tom's daughters too, if they were interested in the farming life. Tom would sort them all out somehow, if it was land they wanted, though how, he didn't know. The farm wouldn't support three families. Barely supported one family, and that only because Eimear was earning a good salary. The farm looked after itself, but Eimear looked after the family. Maedhbh too, nursing away in Waterford.

He didn't know what to do to help, so he did the one thing he could do, as well as he possibly could. The hardest thing was the ditches around fields, with their trees and undergrowth. Anything could be in there. Plenty of things were. Small animal bones, barely visible. Into the bag they went, though how they could be evidence of anything but nature, he didn't know. Better to take everything. That's what they had been told.

Eimear was back at the house, making endless pots of tea, carrying out bottles of water she had gone to the supermarket for. It was a hot one, and the drinks were welcomed. It should be cold. They should need to warm their frozen fingers around mugs of hot sweet tea. Bad things shouldn't happen in the light, bright days of midsummer.

His mother was helping too. Apparently she'd been up at the crack of dawn, baking. The twins were with Eimear, carrying bags of cakes to the tables Eimear had set up past the yard. He's never seen her as a farmer's wife, but it was like the rhythm of it was in her, the work of refuelling those who were working on the land. He wished it were a better harvest.

Joe had wanted to join him. The Guards had said no, though. No children, they said, and Joe had bristled. Of course he's still a child, but sees himself older. Is bent under a weight of something he can't put down.

A sound goes up, a wave of something moving through the searchers. The sub-aqua team has arrived to drag the pond. He'd always pictured that involving a net somehow, not a team of divers in wetsuits and scuba gear, shining powerful lights into the shadowy recesses, startling the fish there. He had told the Gardaí about the pond, first thing he'd said to them, told them he'd shown Joe the pond, sure it was something the boys would have shared. Had been glad Pat wasn't there when he'd said it, could feel shame oozing out of him like pus. Glad though that the boys could swim, Eimear the one who takes them all to lessons, Paudie too when Maedhbh is at work.

He keeps going, using the picker to lift up low-hanging branches, move aside the summer foliage springing out. But there is nothing, nothing, nothing. He wants there to be nothing, because this search, scratching through the ditches, couldn't possibly find anything good.

Keeping to the Shadows

Anything would do. The small hit from a pack of Solpadeine would tide him over, but he has none, has nothing. This is too small a place to steal something in a chemists, if there even is a chemist.

He shivers with the feeling, the nightmare, the memory of something bad, bad, bad. Something telling him to run. He forces a walk. Keeps to the shadows made by the heightening sun. It's hot, and the stink on him is bad.

He can hear the water running before he sees it: the sprayer arcing water out over the field of crops. There is luck he doesn't deserve – work clothes drying on a line in the yard. No one about. He's not clean, but cleaner. The dirt on him doesn't smell as new, as rank. The water pours over his head, over and over, cold and clear, emptying his mind.

Lift This Burden from Me, O Lord

Father Murphy sets down his bag, refuses a cup of tea – the day will float with tea – takes out his breviary.

This is not something that has a precedent. There is no prayer for the safety of the search team, no prayer for the recovery of useful information, no prayer for the missing. This day is a test. Silently, he prays to his God, begs his God to lift this burden from him. Prays again on his selfishness. Lift the burden from the O'Mearas, he asks. Take it from their shoulders and lay it across mine. This is the following I chose, this is the only thing I can do for these people.

He blesses the house, blesses the two parents, pale and frozen on kitchen chairs. In the yard, he says a brief prayer aloud, raises his hands in blessing over those assembled. Watch over them, O Lord, and keep them safe. There's no knowing what they might find out there. No knowing how they might wake up in the witching hours of the night for years afterwards, sweating and crying.

The search teams move out from the yard. He pulls blue shoe covers on over his brogues and follows, in step with Sergeant Maher and his clipboard. Soon he wishes he had worn trainers, his leather soles slipping sideways against their plastic covers. He had wanted to be respectful, appropriate. Should have thrown a pair of trainers in the car. Boots even. He's a long way away from the farm he grew up on, gone now, his older brother dead, gone too soon with a heart attack in his fifties. The next generation have no wish to be tied to the land. He doesn't disagree.

He will go back to the farmhouse in a while, sit with Pat and Maedhbh, and the young Garda assigned to them. He'll be glad to drink the tea, get in out of the sun in his black clothes. For now though, he moves from group to group, patting a shoulder, nodding an encouraging word. He falls into step with Tom Hogan near the pond on his land, a secret circle of water behind trees and bushes. The divers are busy here, the water lapping out of the pond, making mud of the dry soil. Tom is methodically searching through the bushes, tells him there's a foxes' den nearby, tells him to keep an eye out, but it's unlikely the fox will make an appearance with all this noise, all these people.

They walk on together, the heat pounding down on their heads, hammering into the ground with every step. They round a ditch, and the smell hits them at the same time. It's a smell of shit and skunk and something else, something animal and bloody. Father Murphy is ashamed to hang back as Tom leans into the smell, moves forward through it. His brain is untangling this sense memory, as Tom is lurching forward and crying out. A shiver of horror runs through him, taking his breath with it. He pants, unable to move, think, breathe. Tom's words seem to come from very far away. 'The fox,' he says. 'The poor fox. Thieving bastard fox, always taking Eimear's hens, but I wouldn't wish this on him.'

Relief flows into Father Murphy, flushing him bright red and sweating. Not the boy, not the boy, not the boy. Reminds himself that a fox is one of God's creatures too, no less important than a human, but not the boy, not the boy. Tom is still speaking, but not to him. Into a walkie-talkie, speaking with one of the Gardaí, telling him, look, it may be nothing, but this fox was killed, and violently, the head stoved in, maybe a rock or something.

He tells Father Murphy to stand back, the forensic people are coming over to check it out just in case, and Father Murphy feels as though his head is in the pond, cold and underwater, his thoughts swirling, confused. The memory has finally come to him, the smell blossoming here in nature, where it belongs, had been out of place when he smelled it in the confessional the day before, but it's unmistakeably the same. His mind treads carefully along the tracks of logic. Whoever had confessed to him, had smelled of the fox. Had smelled of the fox and was responsible for the fox's death. And had hurt a child. He traces his steps back to where a cluster of blue uniforms stand huddled over a map, calls over Sergeant Maher, tells what he knows.

Shadows Vanish in the Dark

There's a bus stop on the side of the road, the red sign telling him that Expressway buses stop here. Underneath, a timetable. Useless to him; he has no watch, no phone, doesn't know the time. He pulls back into the hedge, squats on his heels. He is good at waiting. He is good at blending into the background. For a brief and blessed time, he thinks of nothing, hears nothing. Some minutes or hours later, a bus breaks the horizon-line. He knows, getting on, that he still smells. People recoil. Head down, he goes upstairs, sits at the back, ready to melt into the city, into the shadows.

He doesn't think about what he's left behind, what he's done or not done. The bus is moving forward, as is his mind. Forward, forward, to where he can fix this sick feeling, take away the nightmares, the terrors. To where he will be alright, if only for a short while.

Night Terror

That night, he walks again. That must be how he ends up at the window, looking out at the still full moon, pouring down light like liquid. He has his GAA jersey on again, but this time, he's also wearing shoes. His trainers, the everyday ones. Not the boots he normally wears to training, whose cleats go clack, clack, clack on the floors like the dog's paws when the nails get too long, and his mam yells for him to put those on outside, at the step, and not be tracking muck all over the house. Not those ones.

As he stands there, looking at nothing, he realises he is waiting for the fox to appear, and when it does, he isn't surprised. It walks up the drive like it's coming home, and again, looks him dead in the eye. The fox is telling him something. He doesn't know what, but he has to follow. He eases open the window, steps up onto the sill, and lands with a scratchy thud on the concrete path that laps the house. No lights go on. No voices call out. He pushes the window to – so he can get back in – without closing it fully. It looks shut.

The fox is still looking at him, as if amused by human behaviour, then it turns its body away from the house. He follows. It is colder than he had expected, and once on the narrow road outside the drive, much darker. Trees and bushes – lush with summer leaves in the daylight – loom over him as he walks, small and alone in the landscape. He knows where they are headed, without knowing how, and he dreads it, and wants it at the same time.

There's no traffic on the top road – hasn't been since the new motorway went in and everyone takes that to get to Cork, or Dublin, or even intermediate places like Middleton or Clonmel. The top road is deserted now, and whenever they turn onto it after being somewhere busy, it feels like a wrong turn, like they've missed a warning sign and will drive off a broken bridge. It hadn't always been like this, though he couldn't remember back to when it was the main road to Cork, so busy that the tunnels had to be built, though there's no need for them now. Now, they can parade the cattle right across the middle of the road without causing as much as a traffic jam. Before, the cattle had to go under the road to get from byre to field, field to byre. Now, the tunnels are abandoned. That's where the fox is heading.

The mouth of the tunnel is a thick kind of darkness that swallows the fox immediately. Joe pauses, looking in, his breathing rasping louder with the echo, or something else. He has to follow the fox, but he has no idea why. He steps in. Despite the dry weather it's like stepping into a river. A place where the sun never creeps in. The spongy, decaying mess of muck and water and moss under his feet surges under his weight and overflows the top of his trainers, soaking his socks. His noise of disgust comes back to him from all angles – his noise, or something else? He keeps looking into the gloom, keeps taking small steps forward. The darkness closes behind him, like a door.

There's nothing visible, until there is: a light, halfway across the dark space. In the light, there's a face, a man's face. It isn't anyone he knows, or he doesn't know if it's anyone he knows, because his brain stops working and he knows nothing any more. His heart stops – he can feel the pain of it bursting inside him – as he sees the man slowly raise his hand and put a finger to his lips.

The air that has left his lungs empty and gasping rushes back into him, filling up the scream in his throat, filling up his whole body, sending him splashing out of the dark tunnel towards the bright, bright moonlight outside, smelling the sweet smells of grass and wheat and hedgerows on a summer night, filling his lungs and running, picturing himself running the length of Pairc Ui Chaoimh, or even Croke Park, hurley in his hand, winning the point. He doesn't stop until he is running down his own driveway and shucking off his wet trainers before tumbling through the window, breaths heaving in and out of him. There is no one behind him, not even the fox.

News Headlines on the Hour

When Joe wakes the next morning, everything rushes back into him as soon as he opens his eyes. Paudie missing; the terrible dream he had in the night; the fox that he knows his da found the day before. He heard his da talking to Mam about it, sorry for the creature that was stealing the hens. That terrible dream. There are boggy socks under his bed, but how long have they been there? Since the night at the pond? He doesn't know, can't remember.

He had slept late and he's hungry; pulls on yesterday's clothes and heads to the kitchen in search of something to take away the aftertaste of the terrible dream. It's loud in the kitchen – Granny must be listening to the radio; its powerful sound is cut with voices he can't make out.

They're all in the kitchen – except the girls who are playing search party in the yard. His mam and his da holding onto each other, his granny saying, 'hush', though no one is talking.

And then he hears it. The voice of the newsreader changes in tone, like when his mam is going to give out to him for teasing the twins. It gets all serious and low.

'In Tipperary, a body has been found during ongoing searches for a missing child. The body was found in a disused tunnel under the R639 near Ballygar. The deputy state pathologist is on her way to the scene, and Gardaí are making no comment yet on whether this discovery is related to yesterday's amber alert…'

For a moment, there is silence, and then everything is noise. His mam is crying her heart out, and his da. Not his da too; he's never seen his da cry. His granny has her hand to her mouth. And he is crying. Crying so hard, as if to push the tears out, scream them away. And he's running, back to his room, away from the terrible thing that is his fault, his fault, his fault for not being there.

Confession

The confessionals glow like mahogany, buffed to a dark shine by the hardworking women who clean the church. Two women from Ukraine, their cheerfulness making Father Murphy feel ashamed. Ashamed of what, he's not sure. Of not doing more, however much he does. They hum around, polishing, polishing, polishing. The wood reflects light, though has no glow of its own. And inside, where he sits, it's clear the wood is darkly stained pine. It's rough, the wood in his centre cubicle. Sometimes, splinters spelk their way into his palms. Sometimes a thing is not what it appears.

He is always listening now. He doesn't expect to get that brutal smell again – the stink of a scared fox – that'll be long since washed off. But the voice. He might know the voice again. In the quiet hours, he ponders how he might deal with that. At four in the morning, when his gritty eyes scan the ceiling in the greying light, he pictures himself bursting from the box, pulling the miscreant out onto the floor, kneeling on him until the Gardaí show up. All it takes to disappear this image is a blink of the eye. More likely, he'll sit there in shock, unable to move. This idea is what stops him getting back to sleep.

A timid closing of the door snaps him back to the present. There has been an increase in the number of confessions this last week. So many of the older people just looking for connection. Or gossip. He has patience for the former. The latter, he's given a few decades of the rosary to give them time to think over their 'Oh Father, isn't it terrible, have you heard any news?' A child dead, and the unsavoury glee of some people. He admits to some uncharitable thoughts. Jesus himself would lose the rag.

He slides back the shutter covering the grill, waits for the 'Bless me father, for I have sinned…' Waits. There's someone there, he can sense breathing.

'Can I help you, my child?' he says: the old words that bring comfort. Silence. Silence.

And then, 'It's all my fault,' and the difficult breathing of someone trying not to cry. Someone young.

'Tell me whatever is troubling you, child, I doubt it's as bad as you think.'

'You're not allowed to say anything I tell you, isn't that right? You can't tell my parents?'

'I'm not. Whatever you tell me stays in here.'

'It's my fault Paudie died, it's my fault. I wish I was dead too.'

The words go through him like hot knives. The shock of it makes it hard to breathe. Surely this isn't the same person as before; surely this child isn't the person responsible. He calms himself, speaks softly.

'Tell me, now, how is it your fault? Is it something you did, or you failed to do?'

'Failed to do, Father,' the voice sobs.

He is more relieved than he could have imagined.

'Tell me the whole story, and we'll see what we can make of it.'

It comes out in dribs and gasps, through tears and snot. There's no culpability here, just a boy who made plans with his friend, and couldn't keep those plans. When the boy mentions the sleepwalking, he's almost certain it's Joe Hogan, Paudie O'Meara's friend. Two youngsters having a bit of adventure, moonlight flits to the hidden pond for a bit of fishing. The sleepwalking meaning he was being watched by the parents; the indignity of being made to sleep on a mattress in their room. No way to let his friend know. Something about the fox, then nothing but sorrow.

Father Murphy wishes the boy could have come to him outside the confessional. Wishes that he could make him a cup of tea or give him a glass of lemonade, though that might be misconstrued. He tamps back the anger that burns in him like the eternal flame, his anger at what the church has been, versus what it should have been. He wishes he could be pastoral towards kids with worries. Help them. Instead he's trapped in a wooden box of retribution, meant to dole out penance like some petty king. What would Jesus do, he interrogates himself grimly, and decides it doesn't involve Hail Marys and Our Fathers, sore knees on hard kneelers.

Slowly, he says the words of forgiveness, tells the boy he is absolved of his sins, neglects the part about sinning no more. Not the time, not the place.

'For penance,' he says carefully, 'I want you to do a really hard thing. I want you to do what Jesus would tell you to do. Go home, sit down with your mam, or your dad, whoever's the easiest to talk to, and tell them what you told me. This thing is not your fault, child; it is the fault of the person who took away Paudie's life. God would not want you to carry this burden, along with the loss of your friend. God has provided us all with loving parents to help us deal with our struggles. This is the time to let them help you with this burden. Go in peace.'

He doesn't close the shutter, listens as the boy gets up off his knees, hears him wipe his face on the sleeves of his T-shirt, hears him gently close the door after him. Quietly, he slides over the shutter. His chest hurts so much, he wonders if he is having a heart attack, feels along his arm for pain. Sadness, it is, just sadness. Sadness like a stone skipped across a lake, skilfully thrown so it touches down once, twice, a dozen times, breaking hearts and lives as it goes.

The Quiet of Night

The house is quiet. The kids are asleep, in bed at any rate. Siobhán has retired to her room with the paper, and the final cup of tea that will send her to the bathroom at two in the morning, leave her restless until dawn, then solid asleep when Eimear comes in with the demanded tea at eight.

Eimear and Tom sit in the kitchen, at the cleared table, now cluttered with mugs, glasses, a bottle of whisky. Neither wants to go to bed, to lie restlessly side-by-side, talk quietly in the dark, turn, turn again, look at the clock with its angry red numbers.

Tom's not a talker. Eimear is chatty, speaks for both of them, usually. She has nothing to say now, either, and keeps repeating, 'I can't believe it,' over and over. The words are like a train on a circular track, like the one Joe used to have, going round and round endlessly. Going nowhere. If she says it often enough, maybe Tom will have the answer. Maybe he'll turn to her, the way he sometimes does, and say something simple, but profound. It always surprises her, the way he cuts through all the bullshit and gets to the heart of the matter. It's like he has an allocation of words for every day, and he doesn't want to waste them. She wants him to say something now, wants him to make sense of this for her. Wants him to cut through the feelings that are lashing her so raw that she checks her skin for cuts, bruises, bleeding grazes. He has no words though, just sits looking into his glass, swirling it, swirling it, the whisky drowned in melted ice slopping up the sides, whirlpooling.

The silence stretches in all dimensions. The tick of the kitchen clock, the growl of the fridge-freezer, other electrical hummings of various frequencies, all grow to fill the void, swell until she has to put her hands over her ears to keep them out, these inhuman sounds.

Tom comes over to her chair, stands beside her, hugs her to him, awkwardly. No words. Just the animal comfort of one body next to another. The kitchen still smells faintly of baking, the rasp of baked jam in the air. Outside, the light shifts from deepest navy to indigo, as the indifferent world turns.

Wordlessly, they stand, bring glasses to the sink, put the bottle away in the high cupboard where it lives, set the dishwasher off on its cycle and walk down the corridor. The twins' door is open a crack, and they are draped on their beds, sleeping off the day's exhaustion. Joe's door is shut tight, and Eimear eases it open, watches him sleep, or maybe sleep.

She remembers when he used to sleep like the twins – luxuriously, as if he'd been dropped on the bed and just slept where he landed. There is something tight about his face where the light bands across it. Asleep, or pretending sleep. She scuffs quietly across the carpeted floor, smooths the duvet around him, pushes back his hair in the way he won't tolerate any more when he's awake. Whispers that everything will be alright. Whispers the lie she knows it to be. Inside her, something cracks, the thing that says everything will turn out okay. It cracks, and as she slips out of the room, the tears that have eluded her all day, as she made tea, made meals no one wanted to eat, kept the twins occupied, watched Joe, all those tears she had kept locked inside, burst out of her.

Tom holds her. Says nothing. Sometimes, there are no words.

Sale of

Residential Farm

Ballygar

Co Tipperary

Description & Accommodation

We are instructed to offer for sale by Private Treaty this residential farm extending to approximately 48 Acres over three folios, together with dwelling house and curtilage.

The lands are located in the townland of Ballygar and have been in family ownership for over 100 years.

The dwellinghouse has been refurbished to a very high standard in recent years, with three large bedrooms, all ensuite, large, open-plan kitchen and family room with study nook. Separate lounge and dining room. The curtilage includes a fenced-in children's play area with swing, slide, and wooden tower. Suitable for families.

Power and water are available to the lands. The farm buildings are located behind the residential dwelling and consists of milking parlour, 2 x 4 bay hay sheds and a number of outbuildings and lean-tos.

The land is set out in two parcels divided by the R639, known locally as the Top Road, with access tunnels under the road. The lands benefit from good road frontage, and have been used for the production of grass and silage over the years but are suitable for all agricultural purposes.

This property is available for sale in one entire lot or in 3 separate lots: Lot 1 being the entire holding, Lot 2 being Land and Farmyard and Lot 3 being the residence (c.140.33sqm).

Maps and further particulars from the sole selling agent, Sean Nugent Properties, available upon request. Viewing is highly recommended. Evidence of finance in place must be shown prior to viewing. Due to a recent family tragedy, viewing will be strictly by appointment. Serious buyers only.

Aftermath

After Paudie's death, Joe dreads everything. People are the worst. Louring over him when he's with his mam or da, asking in exaggerated whisper-speech, 'How is he doing?'. The pretend sympathy makes him want to puke, snarl, sob. They're just dying to ask questions. They'd feast on information like it was chocolate cake – rich gobs of knowledge they could spread around the town.

He takes to staying home when he can, getting out of trips to town, refusing the ice cream his sisters beg for. He likes it when they go into Cork city. He can dissolve into the crowds of strangers, be just another kid dragged into Clarks to get new shoes. He relaxes when they stop in McDonalds for their lunch; it surprises him that he can feel it in his back, his shoulders. There had been a hairy moment when the woman in the shoe shop asked if he was looking forward to going back to school, but he shrugs it off. Shrugs off too his mam's sideways glances.

As the heat goes out of August, he tells himself he won't have to go back to school. Maybe they'll win the Lotto, or his da will get a job on a ranch in America and they'll move; he doesn't linger over details. The night before school starts, he hallucinates – Paudie, alive, telling their friends to stay away from Joe, that it was Joe's fault; Joe's fault for not being there. Joe wakes screaming.

The next day at break, kids shrink away. He senses shaming tears forming, tightens his fists to stop them. One of the other lads sneers, Joe lets him have it in the face. The school is understanding, but he's learnt how to beat down the pain. When he gets his wish, changes school, he finds it's not the escape he dreamt of. Nothing is.

Joe

Joe holds onto the hurley his mam wants to pass on to Ella or Ava, now they're big enough for it, and he has a bigger one. It's an actual fight, her holding one end, he the other. She's calmly asking why he can't or won't pass it on to one of his sisters, but he can see that she is working hard to sound patient when really, she isn't. He can tell that inside, she just doesn't understand why he wants to hold onto this bit of ash with its binding coming undone around the grip, the wood marked brown and faded green from games played and grass slashed at. He can tell too, that she's coddling him a little bit, mammying him in a way that he's too old for now, because of everything. What she's not saying is, don't make us spend money we haven't got on two hurleys for the twins, when we already have one. What she's not saying is, haven't you enough useless stuff in your room already, and by the way, would you please tidy it. What she's not saying is, nothing would have made any difference anyway.

He'd won that round, and had hidden the hurley at the back of his wardrobe, behind the Confirmation suit he only ever wears once, and hangs there forlorn until Mam gives it away to someone on her Facebook group that's looking for a suit. He doesn't take the hurley out, but it's there all the time, like a splinter that the skin's grown over.

When he moves to Cork for college, he packs the hurley at the bottom of a bag, keeps it in the wardrobe of his shared flat. When his flatmate Rory waves it round his head during a party in the flat in their second month, he shoves Rory, who falls onto a girl on the sofa, grabs the hurley off him and slams out into the night with it in his hands, slashing at the bushes by the road, the hurley too short for a proper swing at it.

Years later, when Joe moves in with Claire, a friend of the girl Rory fell on at that long-ago party – whom Rory married and has two kids with now – when they move into their new apartment, Joe casually pushes the hurley to the back of his side of the wardrobe. He winces when she gently takes it out and looks it over, reads the names written on it – Joe and Paudie Forever – asks, 'Who's Paudie?' And holds him when he cries.

Glossary

1. 'putting away the messages' – means putting away the grocery shopping.
2. GAA – The Gaelic Athletic Association, which is responsible for the popular Irish sports of hurling, camogie, and Gaelic football. Each county in Ireland has its own colours, and GAA jerseys in the county colours are very popular, particularly with children who play the sports.
3. Hurley – a stick (not unlike a hockey stick, but flatter) made of ash and used in the sports of hurling and camogie.
4. The delph – means the crockery, or dishware.
5. Confessional/confession box – in the Catholic faith, 'confession of sins' is made to the priest, for penitence and forgiveness. The priest sits inside a wooden box with two or three sections (one on either side of him), and the parishioners can confess their sins anonymously through a wooden grille.
6. An Garda Síochána – the police force of Ireland.

7. Templemore – the training college for An Garda Síochána.
8. Spailpín – an itinerant labourer, a rogue.
9. The Guards – colloquially used to mean An Garda Síochána.
10. Sceilp – a slap.
11. Killt – killed, overworked.
12. Solpadeine – an over-the-counter painkiller containing codeine.
13. Breviary – book containing the religious service and prayers for each day, for priests in the Catholic Church.
14. Lose the rag – become angry.

Names

Eimear – is a version of Emer

Maedhbh – is the Irish spelling of Maeve

Paudie – is a contraction of Padraig, the Irish for Patrick

About the Author

Fiona McKay is a SmokeLong Quarterly Emerging Writer Fellow for 2023. Writes with Writers'HQ. Words now or forthcoming in *Bath Flash, Reflex Fiction, Janus Literary, Pithead Chapel, The Forge* and others. Her writing has been nominated for Best Microfictions and Best Small Fictions. She is supported by the Arts Council Ireland Agility Award and lives beside the sea in Dublin, Ireland, with her husband and daughter. Tweets about writing @ fionaemckayryan

Acknowledgements

I first had the idea for this story when talking to my writer friend Rachel O'Cleary. I had a sudden brain picture of a boy, a fox, a disused tunnel for getting cattle safely under a road, a missing friend. It became a short story of around 2000 words. I submitted it to a few places, where it got good feedback, but not publication. I had feedback suggestions from Retreat West, one of which was that there were too many characters in it for a short story. It was a valid point, and my Flash Fiction brain quietly chanted, Novella-in-Flash, Novella-in-Flash. I planned to write it and made a few notes.

Would I have actually written it, if Sara Hills hadn't contacted me to ask if I'd like to join a group of writers for accountability for longer projects? Maybe? But being part of the group kept me on task, and I got the novella written in time to submit to Bath Novella-in-Flash Award. The group – Sara Hills, Ali McGrane, Rosaleen Lynch, Slawka Scarso, and Rachel O'Cleary – deepened my sense of writing community and gave me so much support. I can't thank them enough – they are wonderful!

I have another reason to thank Sara Hills – at a very critical juncture Sara read the manuscript and gave me great feedback for my next draft. This included pointing out that I was missing a critical scene which had taken place in my head but not on paper! Sara is a wonderful writing friend who is generous with her time and her gifts, and she kindly wrote some lovely words for the back cover as well. Thank you so much, Sara!

I am very lucky to be part of a number of writing communities where parts of the novella were workshopped. Writers'HQ is the writing powerhouse where I got into Flash Fiction – through their course, and then I became part of Flash Face Off – I wrote a number of pieces of the novella using the Flash Face Off prompts as a jumping off point and received encouraging and helpful feedback from members (it was lovely to see 'Looking forward to reading more!') So huge thanks to all the WHQ FFO army (under the leadership of Kathy Hoyle) and in particular – Julia, Mallika, Heather, Fritha, Maria, James, Dot, Mazz, Katie, Kayleigh, Joyce, Noémi, Denise, Paula, Sumitra, Jane, Katie, Paula, Emily, Susan, Tavia, Jo, Karen, and Michelle.

In September 2022 I joined SmokeLong Quarterly Fitness, and again, I used many of the weekly craft tasks to write pieces for the novella. I wrote one novella piece for a Sprint Challenge competition in Fitness and got feedback from Helen Rye – encouraging feedback with some useful suggestions. (I submitted this short piece to Bath Flash Fiction Award, and it made it to the shortlist, which was also very encouraging.) I also wrote some pieces about my main character, Joe, and time, in Sherrie Flick's Masterclass on How to Manipulate Time in Flash. I received encouraging and helpful feedback on novella pieces from all these lovely people – Eleonora Balsano, Jim Latham, Joel Hans, Karen Walker, Joyce Barton, Michelle Morouse, and Shareen Murayama. Thank you also to Christopher Allen, Helen Rye, and everyone at SmokeLong.

I have so many other lovely friends in SmokeLong Fitness, and they are all such wonderful cheerleaders that I would like to try and thank them all here – Claudia Monpere, Elissa Field, Kim Steutermann Rogers, Amy Marques, Dawn Tasaka Steffler, Candice Kelsey, Dawn Miller, Karen Walker, Jill Loomis, Ani Bannerjee, BettyJoyce Nash, and Melissa Llanes Brownlee.

The support and friendship of the Flash Amigas – Slawka Scarso, Denise Bayes, Suzanne Green, Noémi Scheiring-Olah, and Eleonora Balsano – has been essential. We started out as writing-colleagues and have ended up as the very best of friends. Thank you so much, Amigas.

Twitter is my writer-workplace, my office water-cooler-chat-place – I spend perhaps too much time there (@fionaemckayryan) – and I have made so many writer friends there! Thank you to – El Rhodes, Laura Besley, Mallika Narayanan, Audrey Niven, Dan Crowley, Brecht de Poortere, Iona Rule, Iqbal Hussein, Ruth McKee, Rachel Canwell, Kate Axeford, Nicola Ashbrook, Lucy Goldring – and everyone else that I chat with there.

Thanks also to my Mommy Spa Retreat friends – Jenny, Tara, and Katherine – I promise to be around more now this book is finished. And thank you to Carmel Crowley for all the walks and the chats.

I want to thank all at Ad Hoc Fiction and the Bath Novella-in-Flash Competition – Jude Higgins who manages all these and the Flash Fiction Festival too, and also finds time to write fantastic flash herself. Thank you for all that you do, Jude! Thanks also to John, production manager at Ad Hoc Fiction for all his work on the books.

John Brantingham is the judge who chose my Novella as a runner-up in the Bath Novella-in-Flash competition and wrote some very nice words about it in his report. He has kindly allowed me to use them on the cover. Thank you so much, John.

Kristen Loesch is not only a terrific writer, but a lovely friend as well, and not only read the novella in draft form, but also wrote some lovely words for the back cover too – thank you so much, Kristen.

Thank you to Rachel O'Cleary for taking photographs in the area The Top Road is set and giving me permission to use them. Rachel, you really are the best writing friend!

Thank you to Johanna Robinson for the thoughtful proofreading.

And thank you to Jane Ryan for the original cover art that shows exactly the picture in my head.

I could not leave out my wonderful family – Declan and Jane – who give me the time and space to write. Love to you both, always.

In late 2021 I received my first Arts Council Ireland Agility funding. Funding not only buys time to write, but also changes how people see themselves. It made me feel valued – if they were going to give me public money to write, then my writing was good enough and I could call myself a writer. In 2022, I received a further Agility award, and one of the pieces I submitted was from the short story version of The Top Road, and my stated objective was to write a Novella-in-Flash about it. As I wrote The Top Road, I felt encouraged by the fact that I was being funded to do so. This is what Arts Council Ireland funding does, and I thank them for it – I am deeply grateful.

The author received financial support from the Arts Council Ireland in the creation of this work.

the arts council an chomhairle ealaíon funding literature

Printed in Great Britain
by Amazon

42683246R00067